W9-AMO-602
HARRIS COUNTY PUBLIC LIBRARY
LAP

AMAZING
Monty

Johanna Hurwitz

illustrated by

Anik McGrory

CANDLEWICK PRESS

Remembering an amazing friend: Joyce Simon
J. H.

In memory of Dominique
A. M.

First edition 2010

Library of Congress Cataloging-in-Publication Data
Hurwitz, Johanna.
Amazing Monty / Johanna Hurwitz ; illustrated by Anik McGrory. —1st ed.
p. cm.
Summary: First-grader Montgomery Gerald Morris enjoys an exciting year as his class acquires a pair of parakeets as pets, he loses his first tooth, and he becomes a big brother.
ISBN 978-0-7636-4154-2
[1. Schools—Fiction. 2. Family life—Fiction. 3. Pets—Fiction. 4. Babies—Fiction.] I. McGrory, Anik, ill. II. Title.
PZ7.H9574Au 2010
[E]—dc22 2008045982

10 11 12 13 14 15 BVG 10 9 8 7 6 5 4 3 2 1

Printed in Berryville, VA, U.S.A.

This book was typeset in Stempel Schneidler.
The illustrations were done in watercolor.

Candlewick Press
99 Dover Street
Somerville, Massachusetts 02144

visit us at www.candlewick.com

Contents

✿

1

A Sign in the Office

Montgomery Gerald Morris, known to all as Monty, was an amazing reader. Most of the other first-graders in his class were still sounding out words or trying to remember their sight vocabulary. Monty was way ahead. He was already reading fourth- and fifth-grade level books. Because he was a good reader, he wasn't limited to books in the classroom.

He could read everything, and that's exactly what Monty did. He read all the road signs when he went driving with his parents. He read the cereal boxes at breakfast and the advertisements that came in the mail. He read the comic strips in the newspaper and he read the letters that his grandmother sent him. It was because he was such a good reader that it all happened.

One morning it was his turn to take the attendance sheet to the school office. While there, he began reading the notices that were posted on the back wall. There were three people in line ahead of him waiting to speak to the school secretary. That gave Monty time to read the notice about the next scheduled meeting for teachers. It was to be held on Thursday at 3:30. He read about the fundraiser that the parents' association was holding in another month. It would be a bake sale. Then he read a sign that made him jump to attention. This is what it said:

Monty reread the notice two more times. As he stood there, his tongue kept pushing his loose bottom tooth. Monty was one of only three classmates who had not yet lost a tooth, so he thought about it a great deal. But now his mind was not on teeth. A parakeet was a small bird. Monty wondered which lucky teacher would get the free parakeets.

"What can I do for you, Monty?" asked Mrs. Remsen, the secretary. Monty turned to face her. Without realizing it, he had reached the head of the line.

"Here," he said, presenting her with the class attendance sheet.

"Why, thank you," she said, smiling at him over her glasses. "Have a good day."

Monty didn't move. Behind him were two other students with sheets that they were waiting to deliver, too. Monty knew that he should go back to his classroom, but he suddenly had a thought. Just because the notice was hanging in the school office didn't mean that it was addressed only to teachers. No where on it did it say, *I have two birds to give away to a teacher.* Couldn't anyone get those birds? Couldn't he get them? It was a wonderful thought.

Just to be certain, however, he asked Mrs. Remsen, "Can I call that person who wants to give away the parakeets?"

"I don't see why not," said Mrs. Remsen. "Better clear it with your parents first, however," she added, smiling at him.

Monty nodded in agreement. He turned to leave the office but stopped and studied the sign. He repeated the telephone number to himself twice. He didn't want to forget it.

As soon as he got to his classroom he wrote it down in his notebook. His heart was beating rapidly with the excitement of possibly getting the cage with the birds. But even though his breathing was affected slightly, he knew it wasn't an asthma attack. This was a happiness attack, he thought, though of course he didn't have the birds yet.

Having a pet of his own had long been a dream of Monty's. Because he had asthma, he couldn't own a dog like his friend Joey. Joey actually had two dogs! Monty could not have a cat or a hamster or a guinea pig. His friends Ilene and Arlene Kelly, who were twins, had recently acquired a pair of ferrets. Monty couldn't have one of those long furry animals either. All animals with hair seemed to affect his breathing. For a short while he'd had a caterpillar for a pet. It had lived in a jar in his bedroom until it turned into a cocoon and then into a moth and flew away.

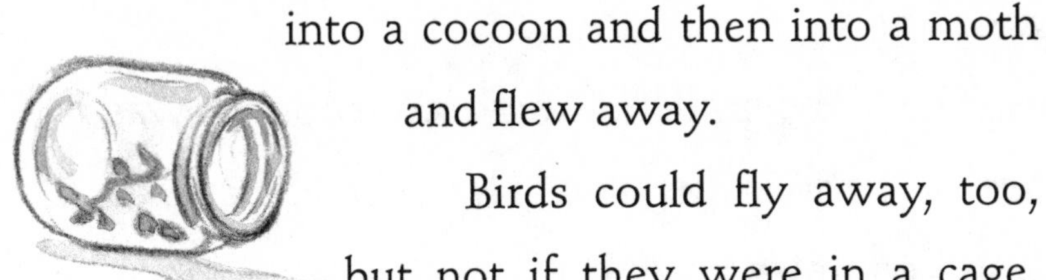

Birds could fly away, too, but not if they were in a cage. And best of all, birds did not have hair. Monty couldn't wait to ask his parents about calling the number. But as it wasn't even nine o'clock in the morning, he had to wait till after school. It was a long, long day. Monty sat in his seat imagining the cage with two birds in his house. Would he keep the cage in his bedroom, or downstairs in the living room?

He wondered if the birds already had names. Suppose he didn't like the names they had? Would he be able to give them new names? Or would that confuse the birds?

"Monty," said Mrs. Meaney.

Monty looked up with a start.

"You seem to be a hundred miles away this morning."

The first-graders laughed. Monty was sitting right in his seat. How could he be a hundred miles away?

Monty blushed. “I was thinking about something,” he said softly.

“Something good, I hope,” his teacher said. “How’s that tooth of yours these days? Is it ready to come out yet?”

“Not yet. But soon,” said Monty. Yesterday his loose tooth had been the most important thing in the world. This morning, he had practically forgotten all about it because he was so busy thinking about getting two birds.

"Try to remember to keep your fingers out of your mouth," suggested Mrs. Meaney. "Your tooth is going to come out any day now. You don't have to keep wiggling it."

All the students in Monty's class had loose teeth. They all spent a lot of time wiggling them even though Mrs. Meaney kept reminding them not to.

The first-graders did their math work. They did reading. They went to the gym. The day seemed to be moving very slowly to Monty. He had never before noticed how long a day of first grade could be.

Eventually the children went to lunch and played outside during recess. Then back in the classroom, Mrs. Meaney read aloud for half an hour. She was reading a very good book called *My Father's Dragon.* Listening to the story, Monty forgot about the birds and the cage for a little while. Then the students went off to the art room, where they were working on life-size self portraits. The only things about Monty's portrait that looked like him were the blue pants and the red-and-white-striped shirt. He was not very good at art. He had written his full name across the shirt. It read *Montgomery Gerald Morris,* and it was such a long name that it took two lines. It was a good thing that on his schoolwork he could just write *Monty.*

Finally the school day was over. Monty's friend Joey lived right across the street from him, so the two boys walked home together.

"You're walking extra fast today," said Joey. "I guess you're in a hurry to get home."

"I am," Monty agreed.

"How come?"

Monty was just about to tell Joey about the

two birds and their cage when he remembered something that Mrs. Meaney had taught the class. They had been talking about proverbs, and one of them was, "Don't count your chickens before they are hatched." Some of the students found this very confusing.

"I don't have any chickens," said Cora Rose.

"Me neither," agreed Joey.

"Of course you don't have chickens," Mrs. Meaney had said. "You don't live on a farm."

"So I can't count them if I don't have them," said Cora Rose.

It took a long time until everyone understood about "Don't count your chickens before they are hatched." But Monty had understood the saying immediately. And now, walking home from school with Joey, he knew that even though the two birds he wanted weren't chickens and they had already hatched, he shouldn't count on them until he had permission from his parents.

"It's a secret," he said. "But I'll tell you tomorrow."

"Why don't you tell me now if you're going to tell me tomorrow?" Joey wanted to know.

Monty shook his head. "Tomorrow," he said again.

They had reached their street. "See you tomorrow," he shouted to Joey, and he ran to his house.

"I've something very, very exciting to tell you!" he shouted to his mother.

"What is it?" asked Mrs. Morris.

So Monty told her all about the sign in the school office. "Birds wouldn't affect my asthma, would they?" he asked. "And they even come with a cage. It would be perfect."

"And who is going to clean out the cage?" asked Mrs. Morris, raising her eyebrows.

"I'll do it," said Monty.

"Well, first of all, I don't know if it's healthy for you to clean out the cage yourself."

"I'd wash my hands a hundred times afterward," Monty promised.

"And second of all," continued his mother. "We should discuss this with your father."

"You mean I can't call right now?" asked Monty. "Maybe someone else will call before me if I don't hurry." He thought a moment. "I know. I'll call him at work." He'd never called his father at work before, but he'd never had such an important reason either.

"Now just keep calm," said Mrs. Morris. "Your dad will be home in a couple of hours. You don't have to bother him at work. Why don't you go play outside with Joey?" she suggested.

"Today is one of his soccer days," Monty pointed out.

"Well then, you could ride your scooter up and down on the sidewalk or read your library book or help me fold the laundry," said Mrs. Morris.

"I'll read my library book," Monty told her with a sigh. This seemed to be the longest day of his life. Waiting. Waiting.

Finally, finally, Monty's father came home. Once again, Monty repeated the news about the sign in the school office.

"What do you think about it?" Mrs. Morris asked her husband.

"Please, please say yes," Monty begged his father.

Mr. Morris was quiet for a moment as he thought. "I suppose if it didn't work out, Monty could make a new sign and put it up in the school office and someone else could take the birds," he said.

"That's a yes!" shouted Monty. He knew that once he got them, he'd never, ever give the birds away.

Monty ran and got his notebook with the telephone number. Then he went to the phone and carefully pushed each button. He didn't want to call the wrong person.

He heard the phone ring three times and was beginning to worry that the owner of the birds was not home. As he waited, holding the telephone receiver in his left hand, he wiggled his loose tooth with his right hand. Then he heard a woman's voice say, "Hello."

Monty took a deep breath, and then he began speaking. "I saw your sign in the office at my school. Would you give your two birds and the birdcage to a boy like me? I'd take very, very good care of them even though I'm not a teacher."

"Well you see . . ." The voice on the other end said.

"My teacher could tell you that I am responsible," he said, using a big word that he hoped would impress the birds' owner.

"What is your name?" asked the voice.

Monty told her.

"Well, Monty," the woman said. "You sound very grown-up and very responsible. However, I'm afraid I've already promised to give my birds to someone who called before you."

"Oh," said Monty. He was filled with disappointment, and his eyes filled with tears. He tried to think of something to say. "What are the names of the birds?" he asked in a quivering voice.

"Yankee and Doodle," said the woman.

"Are they red, white, and blue?" asked Monty.

The woman laughed. "No, they are green," she said.

"Okay," said Monty. "Good-bye."

He hung up the phone. He noticed that his parents were standing on either side of him. "Somebody else called first," he said. "They got the birds."

"I'm sorry, honey," said Mrs. Morris, putting her arms around her son. Then she said, "Monty, what's that you're holding in your hand?"

Monty looked at his hands. There was nothing in his left hand, but in his right hand there was a tiny white tooth with the littlest bit of blood on it.

"It came out!" he shouted in amazement.

"I think you pulled it out when you were talking on the telephone," said his father.

"I didn't even notice," said Monty. He ran to the bathroom mirror to see what he looked like without his bottom tooth.

That night Monty went to bed knowing that he would not become the lucky owner of a pair of birds. But he still had the pleasure of putting his first lost tooth under his pillow. There would be a surprise, maybe a quarter, for him in the morning. He'd also noticed that next to the empty space in his mouth there was another loose tooth. Wouldn't Joey be surprised tomorrow when he showed it to him.

As he dozed off, Monty had a thought: if he lost enough teeth and got enough money, maybe someday he could buy a cage and at least one bird for himself.

2

Three Surprises in One Day

When Monty awoke the next morning, he found not one but two shiny new quarters under his pillow. He ran to show them to his parents before he got dressed for school. The quarters looked so new it seemed as if no one had ever touched them before. Monty knew that most money was spent and re-spent by hundreds of people before and after him.

He brushed his teeth carefully so as not to hurt the little empty space where his tooth used to be. Unless it was toothpaste, he thought he could see the beginnings of his new grown-up tooth peeking through the gum. He wiggled his other newly loose tooth. Monty was good at math, so he knew that two more quarters would mean he would have a dollar. He remembered that he wanted lots of money so that he could buy a bird, and that made him a little sad. If only he had called earlier, he might already be the owner of *two* birds and a cage too.

Joey was a good friend to Monty. So even though he had already lost three teeth himself, he looked with interest into Monty's mouth when the boys met to walk to school.

"Nice hole," Joey said. He didn't ask about the secret that Monty had mentioned the day before. Maybe he had forgotten, or maybe he thought the lost tooth was the secret.

"And I have another loose tooth," Monty showed him. "Maybe I'll catch up with you."

"I have two more loose teeth already," said Joey. "So you probably won't."

He opened his mouth and showed off his wiggly teeth.

"I'll catch up by the time we're grown-ups," said Monty.

"I guess so," agreed Joey.

They arrived at the school building and went to their classroom. Monty was eager to tell Mrs. Meaney and his classmates about how he had finally lost his tooth. But everyone who was already there was crowded together in the back of the room.

"What's up?" shouted Joey, racing to join the others.

"Look what we got!" yelled Cora Rose.

Monty pushed through the crowd of classmates to see what it was that they had gotten. To his surprise it was a birdcage with two small, green parakeets inside.

"I thought you'd all enjoy having a class pet," said Mrs. Meaney.

"These are class *pets,*" Joey corrected their teacher.

Monty stood staring at the birds. He was absolutely certain that these were the very two birds he had wanted for himself. It was hard to believe such a coincidence. The birds were not going to be living with a stranger at all. He would see them every day.

"Let's all take our seats, and after I get the attendance we can talk about the birds," said Mrs. Meaney.

The students all sat down, but most of them kept turning their heads. They wanted to see what the two green parakeets were up to.

"We're the only class with birds," one of the other kids pointed out after attendance was taken. "There are two classes with guinea pigs, and there are three classes with fish. These birds are very special."

"Don't forget that class 1-B has a turtle," Ilene said. Her twin sister, Arlene, was in class 1-B.

"Not a turtle. They have a tortoise," someone corrected her.

"Birds are more interesting than that old

tortoise," said Cora Rose, and everyone agreed. The tortoise in class 1-B had been fast asleep the two times their class had gone to visit him. He could have been a toy made out of plastic for all they knew.

"Can we name the birds?" asked Joey.

"They already have names," explained Mrs. Meaney. "I'm not sure they recognize their names, but I don't want to confuse them by giving them new ones. Let's see if you can guess their names."

Of course Monty already knew the names, and he was about to blurt them out when Mrs. Meaney said, "Whoever can guess their names can be the first class monitor to care for the birds."

"I know. I know," shouted Cora Rose. "Rumple and Stiltskin." Everyone laughed. Just last week the students had seen a puppet show in the library about the girl who guessed the name of an imp who had helped her by spinning straw into gold.

"Rumple and Stiltskin," others shouted out in agreement.

"Good guess," said Mrs. Meaney, laughing, "But it's not the right answer."

Monty raised his hand. "I know," he called out softly.

"All right, Monty. What's your guess," asked the teacher.

"Yankee and Doodle," he said.

"That's amazing!" shouted Mrs. Meaney. "You are 100 percent right. You will be the bird monitor for the next two weeks."

"Lucky duck. How did you guess?" Joey called out.

Monty blushed. "It wasn't a guess. I saw the sign in the office about the birds," Monty explained. "I called yesterday after school. But they told me someone had called before me. I didn't know it was you," he said to his teacher. "Is it cheating that I knew the answer because I called?"

"It's not cheating at all," said Mrs. Meaney. "In fact it's an extra good reason why you should be the first bird monitor. Later I'll show you where I'm going to keep the birdseed. I'll be the one to clean out the cage, but you can sweep up the seeds or husks that land on the floor."

So that was two surprises in one day.

The third surprise didn't come until supper time.

Monty had already given his parents the good news about the two birds he wanted being in his classroom. And he'd explained about his duties as bird monitor. Then his mother said, "Well, Monty. We have some other good news for you, too."

Monty looked up from the string beans on his plate. "What is it?" he asked eagerly.

"Monty, you are going to get a sibling," his mother said.

"I am? Wow. That's great," said Monty, beaming. "Wait till I tell my friends at school tomorrow." Then he thought for a moment. "What's a sibling?" he asked.

"A sibling means a brother or a sister," Monty's father explained. "In a few months your mother will be having a baby, and then you will be a big brother."

"Wow," said Monty. "First I lost my tooth, which shows I'm growing older, and next I'll be a big brother." He paused for a moment. "Will the baby be a boy or a girl?" he asked.

"We don't know," said Monty's mom. "It will be a surprise."

"So that means I could be a big brother to a little brother or a big brother to a little sister," said Monty, digesting all this news together with his string beans and chicken cutlet.

"Right," said Mr. Morris.

"I had three surprises today," Monty said. "Starting with the two quarters under my pillow."

"Three surprises in one day is a lot," his father said. "Now we'll all be waiting for the baby. There will be a fourth surprise, when he or she comes."

"I know what," said Monty excitedly. "Maybe the new baby will be twins. Then there will be five surprises."

"Oh, no," said his mother. "Four surprises are enough."

"Okay," Monty agreed. "Three surprises today. And one to go."

3

Come Back, Yankee

Every student in Monty's class agreed: Despite her name, Mrs. Meaney was the nicest possible teacher. She was always smiling, and she rarely scolded. She was always surprising her students with clever games or treats. Of course, the biggest surprise so far was the arrival of the class pets, Yankee and Doodle. There was not one student in class 1-M who didn't love Mrs. Meaney. In fact, the students had given their teacher a new name. They all called her "Mrs. Nicey."

So the day they entered the classroom and saw another woman standing at the chalkboard, everyone was very surprised. They whispered to one another about the strange woman.

"Do you think Mrs. Nicey is sick?" Cora Rose asked Monty in a soft voice.

Monty shrugged. "Maybe she had to go somewhere like jury duty. My dad had to go to jury duty last month."

"What's jury duty?" asked Cora Rose.

Before Monty could begin explaining, the woman in the front of the room called out, "Everyone in their seats. I don't want any talking at all."

"Mrs. Nicey always lets us talk until the morning bell rings," Joey explained.

"I'm not Mrs. Nicey or Mrs. Meaney, and I said no talking," the woman told them. "I am

Mrs. Bettlebooth, and I am your substitute teacher while Mrs. Meaney is out ill."

"What's the matter with her?" asked Monty anxiously.

"No calling out," said the substitute.

"You," she pointed at Cindy Green. "Get in your seat."

Cindy Green had been hanging her jacket in the back closet. It kept slipping off the hook and she kept putting it back. That was bad enough. Now this terrible lady was yelling at her. Cindy Green started crying.

"Look. Cindy is crying," said Paul Freeman.

"Turn around and mind your own business," Mrs. Bettlebooth told Paul.

"You can't tell me what to do," said Paul. "You're not my teacher."

"I am your teacher for today. And maybe for tomorrow and the rest of the week as well," the substitute told him.

She looked at the students. "I don't want to hear a peep out of any of you now. I'm going to take attendance."

“Peep,” a voice called out from the back of the room.

Everyone laughed and turned to see who had made the sound. Everyone except Mrs. Bettlebooth.

“Silence!” she said in a loud voice.

Cora Rose stood up. She walked over to the birdcage and opened it.

"And what do you think you're doing?" Mrs. Bettlebooth asked her.

"This week it's my turn to take care of Yankee and Doodle," said Cora Rose. "We always do that while our teacher takes attendance."

"Well, that's just dandy," snarled Mrs. Bettlebooth. "Sit down."

"But Yankee and Doodle are hungry," protested Cora Rose, still standing.

"Sit down!"

Cora Rose started crying. She sat down and wiped her nose on her sleeve.

"Now you got two people crying," said Joey.

"I feel like crying, too," whispered Monty.

"Your name isn't Mrs. Meaney but you sure act like a meany," said Joey.

The students all gasped. It was something they had all been secretly thinking, but none of them was brave enough to say aloud. Only now Joey did.

Monty smiled at his friend. He was glad that Joey had said that.

Mrs. Bettlebooth was just getting ready to scold Joey when a small green figure flew out of the open cage.

"It's Yankee," called out Ilene.

"No, it's Doodle," said Cora Rose. However, the truth was that even though the two birds had been in their classroom for six weeks, none of the students could tell them apart. Even Mrs. Meaney-Nicey admitted that they looked identical to her. When they were eating, one of the little green birds stuffed his mouth with seed after seed. The other bird ate one seed and spit out the husk. Then he would eat another. But if the two weren't eating, it was impossible to know which was which.

"Catch him," Paul yelled.

His words were like a signal for the first-graders. Immediately both Cora Rose and Cindy Green forgot about crying. All the other students forgot about the mean substitute.

Everyone's attention was on catching the bird that had gotten out of the cage.

The bell rang for the start of the day. The attendance sheet lay on the teacher's desk. No one paid any attention. Even Mrs. Bettlebooth ran after Yankee or Doodle. The bird circled the desks. He flew into the coat closet and out again. He flew to the window and then up toward the light, circling around and around.

Monty noticed that the windows were open at the top. "Close the windows," he shouted. "Quick, before Yankee or Doodle flies out." He himself rushed to shut the classroom door so the bird would not escape down the hallway.

Even though few of the students had followed her directions, Mrs. Bettlebooth did just what Monty told her. She took the long pole that was used to push the windows open and closed. In a minute, all three windows in the classroom were shut. Yankee or Doodle could not get out.

Mrs. Bettlebooth walked over to the light switch. She turned off the light. The darkened room caught the attention of the students.

"Will everyone please get into their seats," Mrs. Bettlebooth said. She spoke in a softer voice than earlier. She didn't sound so mean either.

"She's probably worried about Yankee or Doodle," Monty whispered to Cora Rose.

"Yankee or Doodle must be very hungry," said Cora Rose. "They always get their dish filled with birdseed first thing in the morning."

Mrs. Bettlebooth looked at the students. No one looked at her, however. Everyone was looking up at the high window ledge where the little green bird was sitting.

"Let me take attendance," Mrs. Bettlebooth said. "Then we'll figure out a way that we can get the bird back into his cage."

As none of the first-graders knew what to do, they were relieved that a grown-up was going to take charge, even if the grown-up was that mean Mrs. Bettlebooth.

"Mrs. Meaney loves Yankee and Doodle," said Cindy. "She'll be very sad if one of them is missing."

"We'll all be sad," Monty pointed out.

"Don't worry," said the substitute. "The bird is not missing. He's just in the wrong place at this moment." She picked up the attendance sheet and called the roll. There was 100 percent attendance except for their missing teacher. Mrs. Bettlebooth handed the sheet to Ilene, who was seated in the front row. "Please take this to the office."

It was not Ilene's turn to deliver the attendance sheet, but no one protested. "Be careful when you open the door," warned Joey.

Ilene opened the door a small crack and slid out. Everyone was happy that at least their bird was still inside.

"Now," said Mrs. Bettlebooth. "How do you think we can get that bird to return to his cage?"

"We could get a ladder and climb up to the window," suggested Paul.

"Yeah. But maybe he'll fly down while we're climbing up," remarked Joey.

"Maybe he'll just come down by himself," said Cindy Green hopefully.

"Maybe not," said Monty. He didn't think the birds minded being inside their cage. They sang and ate and jumped about all the time.

But it was probably much more fun to fly around the room if you had wings and could do so.

The door opened a crack. Ilene slid back inside. "Did you catch Yankee or Doodle?" she asked eagerly.

"No," the students all chorused.

"Not yet," said Mrs. Bettlebooth.

Cora Rose raised her hand. "Can I please go and put birdseed into the cup for whichever bird is still inside the cage?" she asked.

Mrs. Bettlebooth nodded.

Cora Rose took the little cup out of the cage. She got the box of birdseed and opened its spout. Then she poured seeds into the cup and replaced it inside the cage.

"All right," said Mrs. Bettlebooth to Cora Rose. "Go wash your hands and we'll go on with the day's math lesson. Maybe a little later we'll think of another way to catch the bird."

Slowly the students turned their attention to math. Monty tried hard to concentrate, but he kept thinking of Yankee or Doodle sitting up on the window ledge. He looked up at the bird just as it left its perch and flew down—right into the cage. The students and the substitute hadn't even noticed that the door to the cage had been left open. Even the remaining bird didn't seem to have noticed.

Monty jumped from his seat and raced to the back of the room where the cage was located. In an instant, he slammed the door shut. Yankee and Doodle were both inside now. And they were both eating the birdseed that Cora Rose had given them.

Everyone applauded and cheered!

The rest of the school day passed quietly. By dismissal time, everyone agreed that Mrs.

Bettlebooth was not nearly as mean as she had seemed first thing in the morning. After lunch, she couldn't find the book that Mrs. Meaney had been reading aloud, and so she taught them some little poems that she knew in her head. Monty's favorite was:

I never saw a purple cow
I never hope to see one.
But I can tell you anyhow,
I'd rather see than be one.

All the students thought that was very funny.

"I bet she was scared of us," said Monty to Joey as they were walking home. "She didn't know we were such a good class."

"You're right," said Joey. "But I still hope that Mrs. Meaney-Nicey comes back tomorrow."

Monty hoped so too. But he knew that even if their teacher was still out, tomorrow would start off much better.

"So long," he called to Joey as they reached their street. He could hardly wait to see his mom and tell her about the green birds and the purple cow. It was quite a day!

4

An Unexpected Shower

It was a clear but cold Saturday afternoon. The wind came in gusts, blowing bits of grit and dried leaves about. Monty was warmly dressed with a heavy woolen sweater under his down jacket. It made it more difficult for him to move about, but he preferred it to the alternative of staying indoors. He was riding his scooter up and down the pavement near his house. Nearby, the twins, Ilene and Arlene, who lived down his street, were doing the same thing on their Roller-blades. Monty was careful not to bump into the sisters, but once the two girls bumped into each other. Then they both landed on the ground.

"Why didn't you watch out?" grumbled Ilene.

"It was your fault," complained Arlene.

"No, it wasn't," Ilene said.

"Yes, it was," Arlene insisted.

Monty listened to them shouting at each other. When his sibling grew up, he knew he'd never fight or yell at him or her. After all, he'd be almost seven years older, so it would be very different. Arlene had told him that she was eight minutes older than Ilene.

"Big deal," Ilene had responded.

"It is a big deal," said Arlene. "I am your big sister, so you should listen to me."

The twins didn't fight often, but when they did it seemed very silly to Monty. Eight minutes was no big deal at all.

Then the door opened at the Kelly house, and the twins' mother came out. She called to her daughters. Both Arlene and Ilene jumped up from the ground, where they were still sitting and blaming each other for their fall. As he went by, Monty took one hand off the scooter and waved to Mrs. Kelly.

Ilene called to Monty, "We're going on some errands. Come with us."

Monty turned his scooter around and rode toward the girls. Mrs. Kelly had gone back into the house.

"Come with us," Ilene repeated.

"Where are you going?" he asked.

"We're going to the—" said Ilene.

"No. Don't tell him. It will be a surprise," Arlene told her sister.

Monty looked from Arlene to Ilene. "Aren't you going to tell me?" he asked her.

But now Ilene was in full agreement with her twin. "It will be a surprise," she said. "But it's a great surprise. I love going to the—"

"Stop!" shrieked Arlene. "Don't tell him."

"How can I decide if I want to go if I don't know where I'm going," asked Monty.

"Well, you're going to get very lonely if you

stay here riding your scooter without anyone to talk to," Arlene pointed out.

"It's really, really fun," said Ilene. "Say you'll come."

Monty was getting curious. If they were going to the supermarket or a department store they wouldn't make such a fuss. It must be somewhere super special, he decided.

"Let me ask my mom," he said.

"Yeaaaa!" shouted Ilene, jumping up and down. Arlene grabbed her hands and jumped with her. Even though they were still wearing their skates, they didn't fall.

Monty rode back to his house. He pulled his scooter up the couple of front steps and told his mother about his invitation from the twins.

"Where are you all going?" asked Mrs. Morris.

"I don't know," Monty admitted. "It's going to be a surprise."

"Okay," said his mother. "Mrs. Kelly knows what you can and can't do." Mrs. Morris was referring to the occasional limitations on Monty's activities because of his asthma. "Do you have your inhaler?" she asked.

Monty put his hand in his pocket and pulled out his inhaler. It was a small device, made of plastic, that contained medicine. If he had trouble breathing, he put it inside his mouth and breathed. It always made him feel better.

"All right," said Monty's mother, feeling reassured. "Have fun."

Arlene and Ilene were getting into the backseat of their car when Monty got to their house. "Sit in the middle," Ilene instructed him.

"Are you still not going to tell me where we're going?" he asked.

"Yep."

Monty didn't care. It was fun to know that something special was going to happen. It had to be good or the twins wouldn't be so excited about it.

Mrs. Kelly checked that the three children were all buckled in. "Off we go to the—"

"Stop!" the girls shouted in unison.

"We want to surprise Monty," said Ilene.

"Are we going to buy ice cream?" he asked.

"No."

"To the public library?"

"No."

The car started off down the street while Monty made a couple of other guesses.

"To the new toy store at the mall."

"No."

"To the children's museum."

"No."

Monty was running out of guesses. Where could they be going?

"Here we are!" shouted Arlene.

Monty looked around him. He saw a large sign that read CAR WASH.

"Car wash?" he asked, puzzled.

"Did you ever do this?" asked Mrs. Kelly.

"No."

"It's the most fun in the world. It's like going on a ride at an amusement park," said Ilene. "Wait and see."

"Aren't you getting out?" asked Monty, unbuckling his safety belt.

"No. No. Buckle up again," said Mrs. Kelly. "Be sure your windows are closed."

Monty watched as Mrs. Kelly opened the front window and instructed an attendant about what she wanted done to the car. Then she closed her window and carefully steered the car up a ramp. A moment later, the car moved into a dark building. It was sort of like being in a tunnel. All was quiet.

"Now the fun begins," Arlene whispered to Monty.

Then it began to rain. First it was a light shower. Then it began to rain really hard. Well, of course it wasn't raining, Monty realized. But great streams of soapy water were pouring down onto the car's roof and bouncing off the hood. Huge flaps of material

were slapping against the sides of the car. Monty tried to look out the window, but it was soapy and wet and impossible to see outside. It was like being in a huge storm, but they were all safe and dry inside the car.

The only problem was that it was getting very stuffy in the backseat of the car. Monty was having trouble breathing.

"Could you open the window a little?" Monty asked Ilene, who was seated on his right.

"Are you crazy?" she asked Monty. "We'll drown from all the water."

"Just a little," he pleaded.

"No way," said Arlene.

Monty swallowed hard and tried to take a deep breath. It seemed as if there were no air in the car. Neither Arlene or Ilene seemed uncomfortable. But Monty's mouth felt dry, and he was having trouble swallowing. It felt as if a weight were pressing down on him and preventing him from breathing. This was the way it felt when an asthma attack was coming on. It felt as if he were choking.

Monty reached for his pocket to get his inhaler. It was difficult because he was squished between Arlene and Ilene.

"Stop poking me," said Ilene.

"I'm not poking you. I'm just trying to get something from my pocket," he said, gasping for breath.

Mrs. Kelly quickly turned around. "Oh, Monty," she said. "Are you having a problem?"

But Monty wasn't having a problem anymore. He had succeeded in getting his inhaler, and now it was in his mouth. He inhaled, and the medicine immediately went to work clearing his lungs.

Mrs. Kelly honked the horn. "Stop! Stop!" she called to the attendants at the car wash. But because they were inside the rainy building and the attendants were outside, they didn't hear her.

She lowered the window a crack.

"Mom, I'm getting all wet," complained Arlene.

"A little water won't hurt you," said Mrs. Kelly. "It's Monty I'm worried about."

"It's okay, Mrs. Kelly," Monty whispered. "I'm better now."

The car moved out of the building and into the daylight.

Two men with towels were wiping and rubbing the sides of the car. Mrs. Kelly opened the window wider.

"Can you take a deep breath, Monty?" she asked him.

Monty gave a weak smile. "I'm okay now. Honest," he told his friends' mother.

"Wasn't that a great surprise, Monty?" asked Arlene as her mother paid for the car wash.

"Wasn't it fun? Just like going on a ride at an amusement park?" asked Ilene.

"I guess so," said Monty. "Mostly I just go on the merry-go-round when I'm at an amusement park."

“We went on a Ferris wheel with our dad,” bragged Arlene.

“And you screamed that you were going to die,” Ilene reminded her sister.

“I did not.”

“You did so.”

“Did not.”

“Did so.”

“Are you up to having a cup of hot chocolate?” Mrs. Kelly asked Monty.

"Yippee! Hot chocolate!" shouted Arlene.

"I love hot chocolate. Don't you?" Ilene asked Monty.

He nodded. He'd just learned something new. Not all surprises were good for everyone. But it was all right. He felt better now.

5

Two More Showers in One Day

The next day there was another kind of shower. This one was a surprise too. It was a party *called* a shower. The funny thing was that Monty knew about the party and his father knew about the party, but his mother didn't know about it at all.

Monty's father explained to him. "It's called a baby shower. Mom's friends are going to give her presents for the new baby. There was a shower before you were born. Usually people don't have a second shower. But so many years have passed since you were born that we gave away all the infant equipment and clothing. So Betty Wilson decided to give a new shower."

"That sounds like fun," Monty said. Everyone loves presents, even unborn babies. And there always was ice cream and cake at a party, he thought. Only then Monty's father told him that they weren't invited. "Just women," said Mr. Morris. It didn't seem fair. But on the other hand, Monty didn't really want to spend the whole afternoon with Betty Wilson and a bunch of other ladies.

"Here's the plan," explained Monty's dad. "The party is a surprise. So we mustn't let your mom know about it."

Just then the telephone rang. It was part of the plan.

In a few minutes, Monty's mother came into the room where Monty was sitting with his father. "Betty Wilson just called. She has some relatives coming to visit this afternoon and she discovered that her large coffeemaker is broken. She wants to borrow mine."

"Fine," said Mr. Morris.

"Will you take it to her?" asked Monty's mom.

"How about I take you *and* the coffeemaker," offered Mr. Morris.

"I'm feeling a little tired. You don't need me. Just drop off the coffeemaker, okay?"

"Mom, you've got to go . . ." said Monty.

"Why?" asked Mrs. Morris, looking puzzled.

Oops. Monty realized that he'd almost spoiled the surprise. "Because maybe your coffeemaker works differently from Mrs. Wilson's," he said. "You better go and show her." Thank goodness he hadn't given away the news about the party.

"Tell you what," suggested Monty's dad. "Monty and I will drive with you to Betty's. "We'll wait in the car while you drop off the coffeemaker. Then we can bring you right back home."

"All right," said Mrs. Morris with a sigh. "But it does seem unnecessary for three people to take one coffeemaker. Why doesn't she just make tea for everyone?"

Mr. Morris tried to persuade his wife to put on her new maternity outfit before they left the house. "It's such a lovely color on you," he said.

"I don't need to dress up just to deliver the coffeemaker," insisted Monty's mom. Monty and his dad both knew she'd be sorry later, but it would be too late.

They all got in the car. Monty sat in the back with the coffeemaker beside him. When they reached Betty Wilson's, Mrs. Morris got out of the car. She opened the back door and reached for the coffeemaker.

Monty started to say, "Have a good time." Luckily he didn't.

The door opened at Betty Wilson's house and Monty's mom walked inside with the coffeemaker. Even from the car Monty and his dad heard everyone inside shouting, "SURPRISE!"

"Phew," said Mr. Morris. "We almost didn't make it."

Then the two male members of the Morris family went to see a feature-length cartoon that had gotten good reviews. And when they came home, there was a plate with a large slice of cake for them to share. It had come from the shower.

"You really tricked me!" said Monty's mom, trying to sound cross. But she had a big smile on her face. "It was a lovely party," she said, "and it was a real surprise, too!"

She showed off all the gifts she had received for the baby. There were little tiny outfits, booties, sweaters, and soft infant toys. The more Monty looked at them, the more he thought that he should give his new sibling a gift, too.

It was still another six weeks until the baby was expected. He talked about the new brother or sister with his parents often.

He wondered if the baby would look like him and if the baby would like all the same things he liked. Sometimes he put his hand on his mother's stomach and he could feel the baby moving inside. Once he felt a huge kick.

"That was just like a karate kick," Monty told his mom. "I bet our new baby is a boy like me. I can teach him all the karate moves."

"Girls do karate too," Mrs. Morris reminded Monty. "Don't forget Ilene and Arlene both do karate."

Monty nodded. But secretly he was certain that he was going to get a baby brother.

Now Monty went into his room and looked around. What did he have that he could give to a new baby? His books were much too difficult. His games were much too hard. His clothing was much too large. He opened and closed the drawers in his bureau. Then he sat down on his bed, and immediately he thought of something.

He ran to his mother. "Can I have a piece of gift-wrap paper?" he asked.

"Sure. What do you need it for?" Mrs. Morris asked.

"I'm going to give you a present for our new baby, and I want to wrap it up," Monty explained.

"Oh, Monty. That's very sweet of you," said his mother. She had folded up the wrappings from all of the new gifts, so she was able to offer Monty several choices of paper. One had little elephants, lions, and giraffes on it. Another paper had stars in every color of the rainbow. And a third had pictures of a teddy bear doing different activities. Monty liked them all, but the one with the teddy bear was the best.

He took the paper and went back to his bedroom. He put the paper down on his bed and laid the gift on top of it. Then he folded the paper around the gift the way he'd seen his mother do in the past. Of course, the paper didn't stay in place.

Monty went back to his mother. "Can I have some tape?" he asked. "I need it for the package."

Mrs. Morris found a roll of tape and handed it over to Monty.

Monty took it to his room and taped the gift wrap around the package so it wouldn't open.

Mrs. Morris had come home from the shower with all the baby presents and wrappings and lots of ribbons too. That gave Monty an idea.

He went back to his mother. “Can I have a piece of ribbon?” he asked her.

“Monty, what is this mysterious present you are wrapping?” asked Mr. Morris.

“You’ll see,” said Monty.

He took the ribbon into his room and tied it around the gift. There were still a couple of kids in Monty’s class who couldn’t tie their own shoelaces, but Monty was good at tying. When he was finished, the package looked a little lumpy. Maybe he should have asked for a box to put it in before he wrapped the paper around it. Monty considered untying the ribbon, removing the tape and the paper, and starting over. He decided that it didn’t really matter. In one moment, his mother would open it up.

Monty took the lumpy package into the dining room where his mother was still admiring all the new gifts.

"Here is my present for our new baby," he said.

"Oh, Monty. Thank you very much," said Mrs. Morris.

She looked at Monty's father. "What do you think Monty is giving his new brother or sister?" she asked him.

"There's only one way to find out," said Mr. Morris.

Monty's mother removed the ribbon. She carefully removed the tape from the gift wrap so that the paper could be reused again at some future time. She opened the paper. There lay the teddy bear that Monty had gotten

from their next-door neighbor Mrs. Carlton before she had moved away. It had once belonged to Mrs. Carlton's son, who was now a grown man. Monty's mom had washed it in the washing machine, and it looked like new again.

"Do you really want to give your teddy bear away?" asked Mrs. Morris.

"I like it a lot," Monty admitted. "But I think it's a good present for a baby, don't you? Besides, I'm getting pretty old. In the summer I'll be having another birthday," he reminded his parents. "And next year at school, I'll be in second grade."

"That's true."

"You used to think I shouldn't have any stuffed toys because of my asthma. But this bear didn't make me feel sick at all," Monty said. He paused for a moment. "Do you think our new baby will have asthma?" he asked his parents.

"Oh, Monty," said his mother. "We don't know about asthma just as we don't know if the baby is going to be a boy or a girl. But someday, we hope you'll outgrow your asthma. Many people do. And should the baby have it, hopefully he or she will also outgrow it. But there is one thing we know for sure already."

"What's that?" asked Monty.

"No child will ever be quite like you," she said, putting her arms around him and giving him a big hug.

Before going to bed that night, Monty decided not to take a bath. His parents mostly took showers instead of baths. It seemed a very grown-up way of getting washed, and Monty wanted to try it out. His father helped him adjust the water, and it turned out to be lots of fun. It was like standing in the rain with no clothing on and with a bar of soap in your hand. So that made not one, not two, but three showers in one weekend.

6

At Last: The Fourth Surprise

All his life, Monty had been the only child in his family. In the Kelly family there were two children, Arlene and Ilene. Joey had both an older brother and an older sister. Just about every kid in his class had siblings. It was something that kept Monty thinking. He asked Mrs. Meaney if she had any brothers or sisters.

"I have one of each," she responded. "I'm in the middle."

Monty wondered what it would feel like to have another child in the family. He would have to share his parents with the new baby. Most of the time, he looked forward to the big event. But sometimes, he worried that the baby was unnecessary.

Still, lately there had been so much company at home that Monty didn't have time to think about it. First his Aunt Naomi came to visit. She was his father's sister. Then his Uncle Ben and Aunt Kimberly came. Uncle Ben was his mother's brother. Of course, they had all visited before, but only now did Monty begin to think of these relatives as siblings of his parents. Having a sibling worked out for both his mother and father. He guessed it would work out for him, too.

The best company was when his grandparents came. They were his mother's mother and father. They stayed in the guest room, which was going to be made over into a room for the new baby. In fact, his grandfather helped Monty's father paint the room a pale yellow color. Monty helped too. While they worked, Monty's mom went shopping with his grandmother to pick out a new crib and chest of drawers for the baby.

"You won't be able to visit us after our baby comes." Monty worried aloud. "There won't be any place for you to sleep," he told his grandparents.

"Of course they'll visit," Monty's mom reassured him. "Maybe the baby will stay with you for a few nights, or maybe we'll get a sofa that opens up and your dad and I will sleep on it while Grandma and Grandpa will use our room. We'll work it out."

Grandpa went home after a few days,

but Grandma stayed. She was going to help Monty's mom with the new baby. The baby was expected any day now. And in the meantime, she cooked supper each evening and did the laundry so that Mrs. Morris could take it easy. Grandma went to the supermarket and did the shopping. She vacuumed and straightened up the house. She finished knitting a little sweater with a hood that she'd been making. Everything was ready for the baby.

Each afternoon, Monty rushed home from school expecting to hear the big news. Monday, no baby. Tuesday, no baby. Wednesday, no baby. Thursday, no baby. Friday, no baby.

On Saturday, Monty expected that the baby would come while he was home. He went outside and played with Joey. But from time to time he ran into the house to check things out. No baby.

"Isn't this baby ever going to come?" asked Monty.

"The baby will come. Be patient," said his grandmother.

"I'm tired of being patient," Monty complained.

"Me, too," his mother agreed.

"Me, too," said his father.

On Sunday, no baby.

By Monday, Monty had given up expecting the baby. There were too many other things to think about. That day at school, his class was looking forward to seeing a magician who was going to give a performance for all the students. But shortly before the magic show was scheduled to begin, a voice over the loudspeaker in his classroom called out. "Will Monty Morris please report to the office."

Monty was surprised. His name had never been called before. Once Cora Rose was called when her mom came to take her to the dentist. And once Joey was called because his mom was taking one of the family dogs to a vet and no one would be home for Joey when school let out. Monty didn't have a dentist appointment or a dog so he worried a little as he hurried to the office.

To his surprise, his grandmother was standing there waiting for him. She had a big smile on her face and she said, “Congratulations. You are a big brother. You have a baby sister.”

“I do?” Monty asked with surprise. Somehow, he’d forgotten all about the new baby today.

Then he realized what else his grandmother had said. *A sister.* He'd been certain that he was going to have a brother.

"When was she born?" he asked.

"Right after you left for school. Your mother could tell the baby was getting ready to be born. So I drove her to the hospital and your father met us there. And by the time you were eating lunch here at school, you had a sister."

Mrs. Remsen, the secretary, came out from behind her desk.

"Congratulations, Monty," she said giving him a high five. "You're a big brother now."

"Come on," said Monty's grandmother. "I'm going to take you to see your mom and the baby."

"Now? Right now?" asked Monty.

"It's okay," said Mrs. Remsen. "You can miss a little school. This is a special occasion after all."

Monty followed his grandmother out of the school building. Suddenly he thought of something. "What is my sister's name?"

"Your parents have decided to call her Amanda Lee," said his grandmother as they got into the car.

Monty thought for a moment and shook his head.

"That's too long. You can call her Amanda Lee," he said, "but I'm going to call her Mandy."

"It is a long name," his grandmother agreed. "I have a feeling that we'll all be calling her Mandy before long."

"You're going the wrong way," Monty said to his grandmother as she turned the corner. "Our house is down that other street."

"We're going to the hospital. That's where your mom and Mandy are. They won't be coming home until tomorrow."

Monty made a face. "I don't really like going to the hospital," he said. "I can wait until tomorrow to see them."

"Don't be silly," said his grandmother. "You must be curious to see your new sister. And what about seeing your mom?"

"I've been to the hospital three times already," Monty replied. "Twice I went in an ambulance and once Dad drove me. It was when I had bad asthma attacks. So I'd rather go home now, especially since I feel all right."

"I'm glad you're feeling okay," Grandma said. "But actually you've been to the hospital four times."

"No," said Monty shaking his head. "I remember. I only had to go three times."

"Four," his grandmother insisted. She started laughing. "You forgot to count when *you* were born."

Monty laughed. "I didn't forget," he said. "I can't remember that far back."

"This will be your fifth visit. And let's hope all your future visits will be happy ones like this," Grandma said.

"All right," Monty agreed. "Let's go."

And just a few minutes later, Monty got his first look at his sister, Mandy. She was tiny and bald and wrinkled and red.

"Isn't she beautiful?" his mother asked him.

Monty didn't want to hurt his mother's feelings so he nodded.

But his grandma bent down and whispered, "You'll see. In a few days she will be very beautiful. I promise. It's like magic."

Magic. Monty suddenly remembered the magic show at school that he had missed. But the truth was, he didn't care. It was a different kind of magic to have a new baby when yesterday she didn't exist at all. Now he had a sibling and he was a big brother. It was just amazing!